Sorry To Hear About Your Horse

By: Colleen Hollis

Illustrated and digitized by Colleen Hollis
Copyright © 2024 Colleen's Children Line Inc. Ltd.
Publisher: Colleen's Novels Inc. Ltd.
ISBN: 978-1-964768-15-1

I am so sorry to have heard about your beloved horse_____.

There is a bond created when training a horse that is beyond special.

Not only do horses teach you hard work and responsibility, but they can also teach you patience and trust in another being.

Most people can look at a horse
and see their natural beauty.

Only those who truly know
horses can see the effort and
care that has gone into breeding
such spectacular creatures.

We have enjoyed watching you grow your confidence as a horse rider.

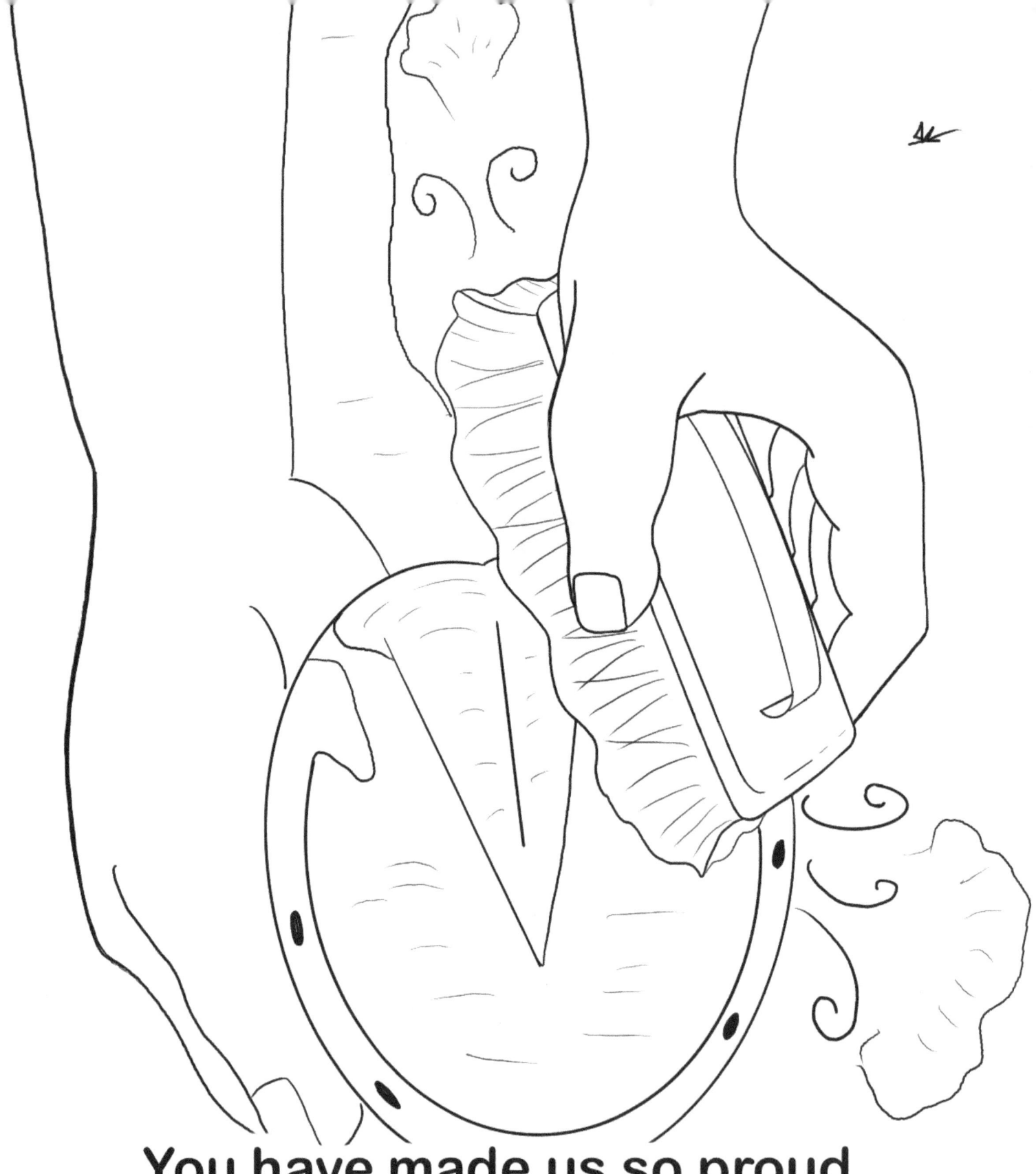

You have made us so proud
with the level of maturity you've
shown while taking such good
care of your gentle giant.

Remembering the many great memories throughout your time together will help ease the discomfort.

When you find yourself feeling sad, know the love you shared with your friend is still present in your heart.

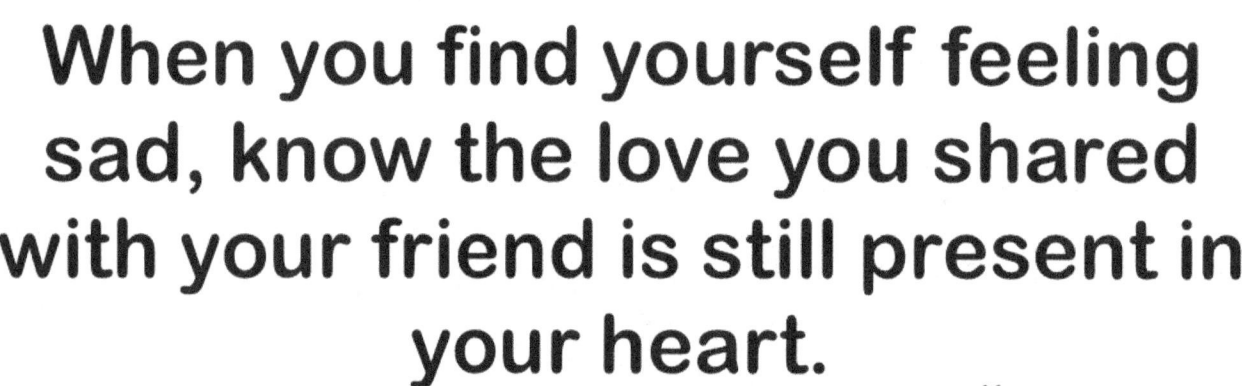

You just have to look within to find it.

So few people are as lucky as
you've been to experience a
bond so special and true.

Reminisce back to sitting with
your beautiful horse just before
sunset, knowing you both gave it
a 110% that day.

Or recall the games you played and the tricks you worked on together.

These are memories that will last you a lifetime.

For now there may only be tears as you say your goodbyes.

However, as time passes, the tears will turn into smiles as you think back on your time together.

By remembering the lessons
you have been taught from this
majestic being, it will show
honor to this beautiful life.

You are never going through this alone.

We will get through this, and anything else that comes our way, as a team.

We love you forever and always.

Love, _____

Friend's Facts

Friend's Name:_____

Friend's Age:_____

Friend's Favorite Food/s:_____

_____

Friend's Favorite Activity:_____

_____

Friend's Favorite Toy/s: _____

_____

Friend's Favorite Person/s:_____

_____

Feel free to write a little note, or share a memory or two.

Sorry To Hear About Your Horse, is one of the books in the children's line from Colleen's Bereavement Line For Children. Colleen's Bereavement Line for Children is aimed to assist in the healing process of children that find themselves navigating the loss of a loved one or pet. Sorry To Hear About Your Horse focuses specifically on those with a horse friend. A name can be added to the beginning of the book, while in the back of the book there is space to write memories about the majestic friend. Followed by a page for "Friend Facts" that can be filled in for a more personal feel.

All animal books in the series are interactive as well, they are in a coloring book format. Art has been shown as a useful tool that can aid in the healing process.